"Hey!" Carrie said breathlessly. "Wait up! I just saw something really strange in the lake!"

Nikki and the twins stopped and stared at her.

"What was it?" Mike asked. He and Max turned to stare at the water.

"I don't know," Carrie said, wide-eyed. "But it was big . . . and, and, it was long, and . . . I think it was a monster!"

"Where?" Mike and Max cried together. They turned to stare at the water.

What's she up to? Nikki wondered impatiently. But before she could say anything, Mike and Max shouted, and pointed at the lake.

"I see it!" yelled Mike. "Neato!"

"Yeah! It's right out there in the middle of the lake!" Max shouted. "Wow!"

Carrie spun around. Then she screamed, and clapped her hand over her mouth.

"There really *is* something out there!" she shouted.

SECRET
IN THE
LAKE

Lorraine Avery

Illustrated by Linda Thomas

Troll Associates

Library of Congress Cataloging-in-Publication Data

Avery, Lorraine.
    Secret in the lake / by Lorraine Avery; illustrated by Linda
Thomas.
        p.   cm.—(Apple Park kids; #2)
    Summary: The bicycle-riding members of the Apple Park Club
investigate the strange appearance of a prehistoric monster in the
lake.
    ISBN 0-8167-1710-9 (lib. bdg.)   ISBN 0-8167-1711-7 (pbk.)
    [1. Clubs—Fiction.   2. Bicycles and bicycling—Fiction.]
I. Thomas, Linda, 1947-   ill.   II. Title.   III. Series.
PZ7.A952Se   1990
[Fic]—dc20   89-5119

A TROLL BOOK, published by Troll Associates

10 9 8 7 6 5 4 3 2

SECRET
IN THE
LAKE

CHAPTER
ONE

"I don't get it. Why are you guys mad at your aunt for giving you a new bicycle?" asked eleven-year-old Nikki Ferris. "That doesn't make any sense." She looked at the two identical, crabby faces belonging to Mike and Max Morrissey.

Mike and Max were six-year-old twins. Even though the pair looked exactly alike, Nikki and her friends had learned to tell the boys apart by their speeds. Max walked just a tiny bit faster than Mike, and Mike talked just a tiny bit faster than Max.

The boys' faces screwed up into even crabbier looks. "We hate it!" they said almost together. "That's why!"

"How could anyone hate a brand-new bike?" asked Carrie van de Hopper.

"Easy!" both boys said at once.

Nikki laughed. She knew that Carrie, who was her age, thought the twins were silly. But Nikki baby-sat the boys every weekday until five-thirty, when their mom got home from work. So Carrie had to put up with them or play by herself.

Max picked up a smooth flat rock lying by the edge of the lake and threw it in.

"You're not supposed to throw it, silly. You're supposed to skip it," Mike said. "Like this."

He swung out his arm and threw the rock flat at the lake. It smacked the water, then bounced up in the air, then hit the water two more times before it finally disappeared.

Apple Park Lake was right in the middle of Apple Park, where the twins liked most to play. Today the sky was cloudy and the park was kind of empty, except for a few people who had rented rowboats. They rowed them along the edge of the shore or lazily dangled fishing poles into the water. Behind the kids stood Big Apple Hill, and the park's petting zoo, playground, bandshell, and carousel.

The twins smiled for a moment as they watched Mike's stone disappear in the water. Then their scowls returned.

"The bike is stupid," Max said, shoving his hands into his pockets.

"Dumb and stupid," Mike added.

Carrie tossed her shoulder-length blond hair. "How can a new bike be stupid?" She skimmed a rock neatly across the water.

"Easy," Mike said. "It's two bikes in one . . ."

"Yeah," Max went on. "It's got two wheels like any other bike, but it's got two seats, and two handlebars, and two sets of pedals. . . ."

"A bicycle built for two!" Nikki said. "That's neat!"

"*Neat?*" Max and Mike both howled together.

"It's stupid!" Max said. "We look like weirdos on that bike."

Carrie snickered behind her hand. "They look like weirdos anyway," she whispered to Nikki.

Nikki glared at Carrie. She hoped the boys hadn't heard what she had said. Sometimes Carrie could be really mean.

Nikki turned to look at the twins. Luckily, both boys were hunting along the shoreline for good skipping stones and had missed the whole thing.

"Well, why do you think your great-aunt Amelia gave you the bike?" Nikki asked. "Maybe she thought that since there were two of you and you go everywhere together, a bicycle built for two would make sense."

"She did it because she's weird," said Max.

"She did it because . . . because . . ." Mike hunted around for something to say about his great-aunt Amelia, but he couldn't find the right word.

"Maybe she did it because she's eccentric," Carrie said.

"What's ecc—ecc—eccentric?" asked Mike, looking interested.

"It's a rich person's word," Carrie told him. "It means different, or unusual. . . ."

"You mean weird," said Max.

Carrie frowned. Then she grinned and shrugged. "Yeah," she said. "I guess we might as well face it. Eccentric does sort of mean weird."

The twins nodded their heads knowingly.

"It's a shame to waste a brand-new bike just because you don't happen to like it," Nikki said.

The dark-haired girl skipped one more stone, then sat down on the shore. "I've got it," she said. "Why not turn one bicycle built for two into two bicycles built for one?"

Mike and Max stared at her. They both frowned. Then Max said, "You can't do *that*!"

"Well, I know *I* can't do it, but Ben probably could," said Nikki. Ben was their friend and he was really good at fixing things.

"*He* couldn't do that either," said Mike.

"I bet he could," said Nikki. "After all, you've got two bicycle seats, two handlebars, two sets of pedals . . ."

"But only one set of wheels," Max pointed out.

"I know," Nikki said. "But old bicycle wheels aren't that hard to find."

"I think you should ask him," said Carrie, skipping a rock across the water. "Ben loves it when you ask him to do something impossible. He thinks he's so smart he can do anything."

■ 11 ■

"He *can* do anything, almost," said Max. "But he can't make one bike into two bikes."

"Well, I think it's possible, and I think Ben can do it," said Nikki. "Let's find him and see what he says."

Nikki, Mike, and Max turned away from the lake. Mike and Max dropped the rocks they were holding.

Carrie sidled up alongside Nikki. "Do you think he's in the gazebo?" she whispered.

"I hope not," Nikki muttered. Then, louder, she said, "We'll see if he's home."

The gazebo was a secret meeting place and clubhouse on the other side of the lake. A long time ago, before the new bandshell had been built, brass bands had entertained people there.

But after the new bandshell was built, the gazebo stopped being used. Trees and thick bushes had grown all around it. No one but Nikki and her friends knew that it was still there.

Ben, Nikki, and their friend Davey had discovered the gazebo at the beginning of the summer. They had broken through the thick vines to the platform where the bands used to play. There they found a trap door as well as a door in the side of the gazebo near the bottom. Both opened into a circular room under the platform.

The room had once been used for storing

instruments, music stands, and folding chairs, but now it was empty and silent. The shrubs and creepers growing outside hid the door from people passing by.

The kids had realized that the old gazebo would make a perfect clubhouse for the newly formed Apple Park Gang.

There were now four members of the gang: Nikki Ferris, Ben Ferber, Davey King, and Carrie van de Hopper. Carrie was a new member, and some of the kids didn't like her too much—especially Nikki. Nikki tried being friends with her, but it was hard. Carrie could be pretty nasty sometimes.

The gang used the secret room to hold meetings, fix up their bikes, and hide their treasury. But Max and Mike were too young to be club members. They didn't know about the secret clubhouse, so Nikki couldn't take them there to look for Ben.

Nikki and the twins followed the shore of the lake around to the park gate. Carrie followed, lagging behind. The day was growing cooler and the boats had all gone in. The sun glinted on the lake's smooth, flat surface. It looked like a big mirror.

Suddenly Carrie came running to catch up with them. She had a scared look on her face.

"Hey!" she said breathlessly. "Wait up! I just saw something really strange in the lake!"

Nikki and the twins stopped and stared at her.

"What was it?" Mike asked. He and Max turned to stare at the water.

"I don't know," Carrie said, wide-eyed. "But it was big . . . and, and, it was long, and . . . I think it was a monster!"

"Where!" Mike and Max cried together. They turned to stare at the water.

Nikki stared at Carrie. Carrie gave her a mischievous wink.

What's she up to? Nikki wondered impatiently. But before she could say anything, Mike and Max shouted, and pointed at the lake.

"I see it!" yelled Mike. "Neato!"

"Yeah! It's right out there in the middle of the lake!" Max shouted. "Wow!"

Carrie spun around. Then she screamed, and clapped her hand over her mouth.

"There really *is* something out there!" she screeched as she started slowly backing up.

Mike and Max both stared at Carrie for a second.

"Well, of *course* there is, dummy," Max said. "*You* were the one who told us about it. . . ."

Nikki squinted, but all she could see was a sparkling shimmer on the lake.

"I don't see anything," she said.

"Keep looking," Mike said.

"It just dove down," Max said. "Wait a minute."

"I saw it . . ." Carrie stuttered. "I saw a monster . . . I really did."

"Wow," Mike said. "A real live sea monster . . . like the Loch Ness Monster, I bet."

Nikki turned to look at Carrie. Carrie's face had gone white as a sheet. "Did you really see something, Carrie?" Nikki demanded. "Or did you just make it up to scare the boys?"

Carrie had turned very pale.

"I really saw it. Just now I did," she said. Her voice was very high and trembly. "Before, when I said that, I was just making it up, but then when the boys looked, there it was. It was really out there. . . ."

Carrie turned on her fancy leopard-print flats and ran out of the park.

"There's a monster in the lake!" they heard her yell as she disappeared out of the gate. "There's a monster in the lake!"

A family just leaving the park stared at Carrie, then laughed as she ran past. They thought she was playing a game.

Nikki knelt down in front of Mike and Max. Both of them had their eyes fixed on the glistening water.

"Now, tell me the truth," Nikki said. "Did you really see something out there?"

"Yup." Mike nodded so hard his blond hair fell across his eyes.

"Did it really look like a sea monster?"

"Yup," both boys said solemnly.

"What does a sea monster look like?" Nikki asked.

"It was big, with a long neck . . ." Mike said.

". . . And it had a round, humpy back," Max added.

". . . And it was all shiny and black," Mike went on.

"It was really neat," Max said. "Why did Carrie run away screaming like that?"

"I think Carrie just made up the monster to scare you," Nikki said carefully.

"No," said Mike and Max together in disbelief.

"It was really there," Mike said firmly.

"We saw it," Max added.

Nikki sighed. "I think we'd better go tell Ben what just happened. Then maybe we can ask him about your bike too."

The three of them hurried out of the park gate and over to Ben's house across the street. They found him in the garage, clanking away on the frame of his new racing bike. He was younger than Nikki, but bigger. When he saw them, his freckled face lit up in a big, friendly grin.

"Ben!" Nikki said breathlessly. "Guess what happened? Carrie told the boys she saw a monster in the lake. She just told them that to scare them, and—"

"But there really *was* a monster," Mike said.

"We saw it. Honest," Max cried.

"Really?" Ben stood up and gave Nikki a quizzical look. He didn't know whether to believe the twins or not. "What kind of monster?"

"Come on," Mike said, taking his hand. "Come see for yourself. It had a long neck and a little head and a humpy back . . . ."

"And they say it was shiny and black," Nikki said.

"Jeez." Ben grinned. "That's neat!" Then he frowned. "I mean, that's terrible! But are you sure? Maybe you just *thought* you were seeing a monster. Maybe you guys made a mistake!"

"We did not!" Mike said indignantly. "Carrie saw it too."

"She *did* look like she really saw something after the twins pointed it out to her," Nikki told Ben. "She ran screaming out of the park. It's not like her to act that crazy just to make a joke."

"Well, let's go see, then," Ben said.

The three of them walked back to the lake. They stared at it for a long time. But no lake monster with a long neck and humpy back appeared. There wasn't even the tiniest ripple, much less a big black monster.

"I've got to get home for dinner," Ben said finally. "I don't know about this monster. . . ."

"It's there!" Mike said loudly. "Ask Carrie!"

"You just have to wait long enough and it'll come back!" Max insisted.

Ben and Nikki looked at each other. They didn't know what to think.

"Well, listen," Ben said, winking at Nikki.

"You kids keep watching. I have to get home. See you later!"

Nikki watched Ben leave the park. The twins kept their eyes glued to the surface of the lake.

"I'd better get you guys home too," Nikki said reluctantly. "It's nearly five-thirty. We can keep looking tomorrow."

The three of them walked slowly away from the lake. The twins kept turning their heads back toward the water. Nikki was the only one watching where they were going. She had to hold on tight to Max's and Mike's hands to keep them from banging into trees or benches.

"*Hey!*" Mike said. "Look quick!"

Nikki spun around. She saw a faint ripple on the lake. Was it a fish?

"Rats!" said Max. "You missed it."

"Let's go back and watch some more!" Mike said, yanking on Nikki's hand.

"We really have to get home," she replied. To change the subject and get the boys to think about something else, she added, "You know what we forgot? We forgot to ask Ben about fixing your bike."

"Who cares about a stupid bike," Max said excitedly, "when there's a real live monster in Apple Park Lake!"

CHAPTER
TWO

First thing the next morning, Mike and Max raced over to Nikki's house. They banged on her front door until Nikki opened it.

"You'd better come to the park with us, Nikki," Max said. He reached out and grabbed her hand.

"But it's only nine-thirty." Nikki yawned. "I haven't even eaten my breakfast yet." She turned around to go back inside.

"Have a hot dog for breakfast," Max said, following her into the living room. "Buy one from Ben's uncle. Hurry up!"

"Yeah!" Mike said. "There's millions of people there already, looking at the monster!"

"Millions?" Nikki smiled, putting on her sneakers. "There's never millions of people in Apple Park."

"Well, there's millions there now!" Mike said. He grabbed Nikki's hand and dragged her out of the living room and onto the porch.

Then she stopped. "Hold on, guys!" she said. "I've got to get my bike!"

Mike and Max let go of Nikki. She ran around the house to the garage. It wasn't until she wheeled her bike back to the sidewalk that she saw what the twins had been complaining about the day before.

Lying on the grass by the walk was the strangest-looking bike she'd ever seen. It was just the way Max and Mike had described it—two wheels, like every other bike, but this one was long and had two handlebars, two seats, and four pedals!

She had to put her hand over her mouth to keep from laughing when the boys clambered aboard. Mike sat in front. Max was right behind him. They had a hard time trying to get the bike going. When one pedaled, the other didn't. They wobbled down the driveway and pulled out onto the sidewalk.

"See?" Max snapped when the bike tipped over. He managed to catch himself before both of them fell off. "This bike is dumb and stupid. Right?"

"You could always walk it to the park." Nikki pulled her bike up next to them.

"No way!" Mike and Max said together.

"That would look even stupider," Mike added, pouting.

The twins got back on, counted to three, and started pedaling. Finally, all three of them managed to get to Apple Park.

Nikki could hardly believe her eyes when they rode through the front gate. The park was jammed with people. There were people standing four deep around the edge of the lake. There were people in the bandshell with telescopes and binoculars. There were even people perched up in the trees with cameras and zoom lenses hanging around their necks.

The first person they saw whose eyes weren't fixed on the lake was Ben's uncle Frank.

"Hi there, kids," he called out to them.

Uncle Frank lived with Ben's family and ran a hot dog stand in the park. It was called Uncle Frank's Franks. He liked to treat Ben and his friends to free hot dogs and sodas.

Nikki had never seen such a long line at Uncle Frank's hot dog stand. Uncle Frank looked very happy.

"Some crowd, eh?" he said, waving his arm at all the people in the park.

Mike and Max were pushing their bicycle ahead through the people, so Nikki waved at Uncle Frank and went after them.

The boys moved steadily through the crowd until they were close to the rowboat rental dock. About twenty people were standing on the end of the dock waving money at Mr. P and shouting at him.

Mr. P was the park keeper. His real name was Spyros Papadopoulos, but none of the kids could pronounce it. Neither could a lot

of their parents, so everyone just called him Mr. P.

Mr. P was in charge of renting boats, but today he wouldn't let people take any out on the lake. "If there's a monster out there, folks," Nikki heard him tell one man and his big family, "I wouldn't want to be responsible for what happens. After all, it could be dangerous, who knows?"

The father didn't look very happy. One of his kids started crying. "I wanna go out in a boat, Daddy! I wanna go out in a boat!"

But the boats stayed roped together at the edge of the dock. No one could persuade Mr. P to let them out on the lake today.

Then Nikki caught sight of someone riding around the lake she wished she hadn't seen. His nickname was Wheels Gilligan, and if the Apple Park Gang had a sworn enemy, Wheels was it. He liked to frighten the little kids who played in the park by riding straight for them with his scary-looking mountain bike.

As Wheels rode closer, Nikki saw that he had two big cardboard boxes strapped to his bike, and he was flapping a T-shirt in front of him.

"Get your T-shirts!" Wheels yelled. "Get your Bessie the Lake Monster T-shirts! While they last, folks!"

Nikki saw a picture on the front of the T-shirt of an animal that looked like a black brontosaurus. It was taking a bite of an apple. She wondered how Wheels had gotten a T-shirt of a lake monster printed so fast.

"Only ten dollars!" Wheels hollered. "Get your Bessie T-shirt now!"

Ten dollars! Nikki thought to herself. That's a lot of money!

Nikki followed the twins through the crowd, but since she was still watching Wheels, she smacked right into Davey King and Ben Ferber.

"Whoa!" Davey said. "Not so fast, Nikki. You'll knock someone into the lake, where they'll be eaten by . . ." Davey's eyes grew big and round. He pretended to look scared.

". . .I know. A ferocious lake monster!" Nikki said, laughing.

"It sure does look like all these people expect something to happen," Davey said. "The park's never this crowded, not even on the Fourth of July."

"I'll bet Carrie went screaming about the monster through the whole town," Mike said.

"Yeah," Max agreed. "She sure ran out of here yelling pretty loud yesterday."

"Well, Uncle Frank is sure happy," Ben said. "Even if there isn't any monster, he's selling more hot dogs in one day than he normally sells in a whole year."

"Wheels Gilligan isn't losing out, either," Nikki said, shaking her head. "Did you see him selling those T-shirts for *ten dollars*?"

"I think his uncle's in the T-shirt business," Dave said. "He must have had a bunch of dinosaur T-shirts lying around. Dinosaurs look enough like lake monsters for Wheels, I guess."

"Did anyone see the monster yet today?" Max asked excitedly.

"Nope," Ben said. "Maybe it doesn't like crowds."

"Maybe it doesn't even exist," Nikki said firmly. "I think Carrie made the whole thing up."

"No way!" said Mike. "We saw it!"

Davey looked down and noticed Mike and Max's new bike for the first time.

"Hey, guys!" he said, his face breaking into a smile. "Look at that bike!"

"It's dumb and stupid," muttered Mike.

"No, it isn't," said Davey. "It's a tandem bike. They're neato!"

"They're dumb-o," Max grumbled.

"C'mon, show me how it handles," Davey said.

"Okay," said Max. "But you'll see! It handles dumb and stupid."

Mike and Max climbed onto the bike. After three bad starts, they wobbled off. Two minutes later, the bike flopped over on the grass. But the twins got back on and started again. They wanted to look good on the bike for Davey.

Davey was the champion bike racer in Ap-

ple Park. He'd beaten Wheels Gilligan in the Big Apple Bike Event the month before. As far as Mike and Max were concerned, Davey was a world-class hero.

But even though they were trying really hard, they just couldn't get the bike to work right. Nikki smiled as she watched them wobble around the park, trying to look as cool as possible. Finally, after circling the park three times and falling off their bike five times, the twins gave up.

Mike looked as if he were about to cry, and Max gave the front wheel a hard kick as they dropped the bike onto the grass near Ben and Nikki.

"Hey, guys," Davey said. "Don't worry, you'll figure it out."

"No we won't!" said Max glumly.

"I had an idea yesterday," Nikki said. "I thought since you know all about bikes and how to build things, Ben, maybe you could make this bike for two into two bikes for one."

Ben stopped and stared at the bike. Then he grinned from ear to ear. "Yeah! That's a great idea, Nikki."

Mike and Max didn't look too happy, though.

"Aw, you can't do that," Max said.

"It's too hard," Mike said.

"No, it's not," Ben said, getting down on his hands and knees next to the bike. "Let's see . . . all you need is another head tube, another seat stay, another chain stay ... maybe another chain, and a brake set ... two wheels—a front and a back ..."

"See?" Mike said. His face started looking crabby again. "It's impossible!"

"No, it's easy," Ben said. He flipped the bike up so he could get a better look at it. Then he squinted at the frame.

"It's too hard," Max said. "Where're you planning to get all that stuff from, anyway ... even if you could do it?"

"Junk for bikes is no problem," Davey said. "I've got a whole room full of junk. And besides, people throw old bikes away at the dump."

"Yeah, but how're you gonna get it all to fit together?" Mike asked.

"And how're you gonna get this one apart?" Max said.

"No problem," Ben said. "We'll just saw the back tube and the down tube off the front seat tube." He ran his hands along the metal frame to show them where he would cut. Nikki watched carefully. She wanted to be sure he knew what he was doing. It was a brand-new bike, after all. She didn't want to get the twins into trouble.

"I'm telling you guys," Ben said to the twins, "it'll be a cinch." He flipped the bike over so that it was resting upside down on the two seats.

Mike and Max stood shoulder to shoulder, looking worried. "You mean it'll be a cinch sawing it apart, I bet," said Max. "I bet you won't be able to get it together again."

"Are you nuts?" Ben stood up. "I can do anything—especially when it comes to working on bikes. I even have a welder that my dad showed me how to use. No problem!"

"What if it doesn't work?" Max asked.

Nikki sighed. "I'm sure Ben wouldn't try it if he didn't think he could do it," she said to Max. "And you hate it like it is, right?"

Mike and Max nodded.

"So maybe it's worth a try."

Both twins looked at the bike glumly. "Okay," they said together finally.

"Hey, look!" Nikki said, pointing to the dock. "There's Julia Forbes."

"She has a TV camera with her too!" Max said.

"Let's go see what's happening," Davey said. "Maybe she'll want to interview you guys. After all, you're the ones who saw the monster, right?"

"Right!" Max said. "But Carrie saw it too."

"I wonder where Carrie is?" Nikki asked.

"Well, I haven't seen her," said Ben. "But I'm not surprised. Maybe she's scared!"

The five of them made their way through the crowds packed along the edge of the lake.

Julia Forbes was a television news reporter

from WAPG. She was interviewing Mr. P at the end of the dock.

"Is it possible that Bessie the Lake Monster is a hoax?" she asked. She held the microphone out to Mr. P.

"Well, I don't know about that, Ms. Forbes," Mr. P said slowly. "I don't know how anyone got the idea there was a monster in that lake in the first place, much less that her name is Bessie."

"Isn't it a bit unusual for hundreds of people to show up in the park on Saturday morning claiming they heard about a monster?"

"It sure is," Mr. P said.

"Any ideas on who saw this monster first?"

"Nope," Mr. P said. "But I sure would like to see it myself—if it's out there. I hear it's supposed to have a long neck and a little head, and a big, shiny, round back."

"Sounds scary to me." Julia Forbes smiled into the camera. "We'll be back with an update on the Apple Park Lake monster tonight at six o'clock. This is Julia Forbes, live from Apple Park Lake."

"Hey! Ms. Forbes!" Mike yelled. He and Max pushed their way through the crowd. "Ms. Forbes! Talk to us!"

But it was no use. Julia Forbes and the camera crew were already getting into their van. The kids hadn't even gotten close to the dock before the truck drove away.

"Don't worry, guys," Ben said. "We'll catch her the next time she comes to interview people. Let's go over to my house now and get started on your bike."

"If Ben doesn't have all the right parts," Davey said, taking off in the direction of his own home, "stop by my house. I've got a whole collection!"

"What about the monster?" Mike asked.

Ben looked at Nikki and grinned. "How about this? You guys stay here and watch for the monster. I'll take your bike home and get to work."

"But what if you miss the monster?"

"That's okay with me." Ben shrugged. "Any monster worth seeing would have shown up by now. Besides," he laughed, "I'm only interested in the kind that hangs around all the time."

Ben wheeled the tandem bike out of the park while Nikki, Mike, and Max found a spot near the lake to sit and monster-watch.

But the monster never appeared, and after a little while the twins got restless and bored. Nikki decided to take them home and head back to her own house.

"Too bad about the monster," Nikki called to the twins as she watched them go into their house. "Maybe next time."

"There were too many people there," Mike said, disappointed.

"I don't think she likes strangers," Max agreed.

Nikki rode her bicycle home, thinking about all the people at the lake. "It's probably nothing, and I bet there's a good reason," she said to herself, "but I wonder where Carrie van de Hopper's been all day?"

CHAPTER
THREE

Since the next day was Sunday, Nikki left her house bright and early. The gang always met at the gazebo on Sunday mornings, especially if they were working on something. Now that Ben was rebuilding the twins' bike, Nikki was sure that everyone would show up.

As she crossed the street across from the park, she ran into Ben. He was pushing the twins' bike with one hand. In the other he had a lumpy satchel that clanked as he walked. He wore his backpack, and that was lumpy too. A long rope was looped around his neck and under one arm. There was a pair of plastic goggles stuck on the top of his head.

"You look like a very strange clown," Nikki said when she saw him, "or a junk man who's lost his cart."

"I didn't really get any work done on the bike last night. I want to work on it at the gazebo," Ben said, "so I need all my tools and stuff."

The two of them went into the park. Hardly anybody was there today. One or two joggers were running along a path.

Once inside the gazebo, Ben dumped the lumpy bag on the floor. Then he shrugged off the backpack and let the twins' bike rest against the wall.

"I charged up my cordless drill overnight, in case I need it," Ben said.

Nikki watched Ben unpack the rest of his stuff. He laid out a hacksaw, a file, his set of adjustable crescent wrenches, a hammer, pliers, screwdriver, and two pairs of vise grips.

"Rats." Ben held up a small metal container with a squirt top. "It leaked."

"What is it?" Nikki took a step back. Whatever it was, it looked messy. It had leaked through the cap and left a big slimy stain on his backpack.

"It's penetrating oil," Ben said. "You squirt a few drops on a rusted nut, and it pops loose."

"Well, it's penetrated your backpack too," Nikki pointed out. "You'll have to get a new one for school in the fall. Otherwise your sandwiches will taste pretty awful."

"You're a wise guy, you know that, Nikki?" Ben sounded angry, but he laughed and wiped the oil off his hands onto some leaves.

"I guess I am," Nikki agreed. Then she looked again at all Ben's tools. "It looks like you've got most of the tools you'll need," she said. "But what about parts?"

"Well, I have a spare chain and chainwheel, all the right nuts and bolts and hose clamps, and an extra crankset," Ben said. "But I still need a few little things. . . ."

"Oh, you mean little things like wheels, frames, and brakes?" Nikki said.

"Well, yeah!" Ben grinned. "But that stuff isn't so hard to find. I just didn't have time to go to the dump. I was hoping I could send the rest of the gang on a scavenger hunt."

"They should be here soon," Nikki said, looking at her digital watch. "It's after nine-thirty."

"Okay," Ben said. "Meanwhile, I can get started."

"What can I do?" Nikki asked, picking up a wrench.

Ben laughed. Nikki had a reputation as the class brain, but Ben knew that even though she was a whiz at math and computers, she didn't have any idea how to use a screwdriver.

"Just watch." Ben bent over the bicycle chain.

Soon Ben had taken off the chain. As Nikki watched, she found herself wondering about the lake monster. Had the twins really seen it? And if they had, what kind of creature was it? Where could it have come from?

Ben was unscrewing the back handlebars from the seat post when suddenly he stopped. "I just realized," he said. "I need another handlebar stem and a bunch of headset bearings."

Nikki looked at him blankly. "Where do those come from?"

"I've got some old headset bearings in my garage at home." Ben wiped his hands on his jeans. "Let's go."

"You just want me along to carry stuff, right?" Nikki asked, following him out of the gazebo.

Ben laughed and took off around the end of the lake. Nikki had a hard time keeping up with him. He ran so far ahead of her, she could barely see him as he leapt over two of the park benches.

She was about to call to him to wait up when in the distance she saw him stop midstep. He seemed to be staring at the lake. Then he turned and waved to Nikki.

"Nikki!" Ben yelled. "It's Bessie! The lake monster!"

Nikki stared at him in surprise. Then she turned to look at the lake. Its surface was as still as always. She turned back to Ben.

"I don't see anything," she called. She ran to catch up with him.

"I saw it!" Ben said when Nikki joined him by the benches. "It had a long, skinny neck and a little head! And a kind of rounded back

sticking up out of the water! I can't believe you didn't see it!"

Nikki had never seen Ben so excited. His face was red and his eyes were really wide. He was looking around to see if anyone else had noticed the monster. But there was no one else in the park. The joggers from that morning had all gone home.

"It was definitely there, Nikki," he said to her. "I swear it was!"

Nikki frowned. "Whatever it was, it's gone now."

"I'll get the rest of the gang!" Ben said excitedly. "You stay here and watch!"

"What about the headset bearing?" Nikki asked.

It was too late. Ben was already careening out the park entrance onto the street. Nikki sighed, and took another look at the calm, glassy surface of Apple Park Lake.

Fifteen minutes later Ben was back with Davey and Carrie. Uncle Frank was with them too. He wheeled his hot dog wagon to the edge of the lake.

"Did you see it again?" Carrie asked insistently.

"Nope," said Nikki. "I didn't see it at all. Ben did. All I saw was five ducks and a bullfrog."

"Keep watching," said Davey. "Carrie called Julia Forbes at WAPG. The crew'll be here any minute."

"Aren't you kids going to stay here?" Uncle Frank called out as the gang disappeared around the edge of the lake.

"Er . . . we're going to keep watch from over here," Ben called over his shoulder. Ben didn't want to let on that they were really headed for their clubhouse. No one else knew about the gazebo except Mr. P. "We're going to hide in the bushes . . . just in case Bessie is a shy monster," he said.

He hated not telling his uncle the whole truth, but it wasn't as if they were doing anything wrong.

The gang members piled into the clubhouse and closed the door behind them. It was a relief to be inside, where no one could spot them.

"Oh, boy!" Davey let out a whistle when he saw the pile of junk on the floor.

"Oh, no!" Carrie said when she saw what a mess the twins' bike was in. "What did you do to it?"

"Don't worry," Ben said. "I have to take it apart to get it back together again, right?"

"I guess," Carrie said. She wrinkled her nose at the messy pile of sawed-off metal parts.

"Forget about the bike for a minute," Davey said to Ben. "Where did you see the monster?"

"In the lake, of course," Ben said impatiently.

"No one believed me," Carrie said with a sniff. "That's why I didn't come to the park yesterday. I knew you'd all say I made it up."

"But you did," said Nikki. "You admitted it to me yourself!"

"Well . . ." Carrie looked a little guilty. "At first I just pretended I'd seen a monster, as a joke. But when Mike and Max looked, so did I. And it was there! Now you know I wasn't lying because Ben saw it too!"

"But I was right behind him," Nikki said. "And I didn't see it!"

"Okay, so we think there might really be a monster," Davey said. "There's no point in fighting about it. We'll just have to wait and hope we can spot it again when other people are looking too. Now, what do we need for the bike, Ben? We'd better get it made into something the twins can ride."

Ben gave them all a quick rundown of what he needed. He also told them where to look.

"First check the junkyard, and that old vacant lot behind the grocery store. As a last resort, you can stop by the bicycle shop off Maple Street—maybe they have some stuff lying around in the garage. Try not to pay more than fifty cents for anything."

"Do we have any money in the treasury?" Davey asked. The treasury was what the gang had saved for snacks and other supplies for the clubhouse.

"Yup," Nikki said. "But only four dollars . . .

and we need that to buy cookies with." She gave Davey and Carrie a little smile.

They all laughed at the upset look on Ben's face.

"Don't worry, Ben," Davey said as the rest of the gang headed out of the gazebo. "We'll use that four dollars to fix up a really neat bike for the twins."

Nikki was in the lead as they came around the edge of the lake. Suddenly she stopped.

"Wow!" she said. "Look at all the people!"

Sure enough, the park was filled with people again. The WAPG news van had arrived and most of the crowd had gathered around it. Uncle Frank was beginning to do a good hot dog business, too, and Wheels Gilligan was back with his two boxes of T-shirts.

Mike and Max ran up to the gang. "Did you fix our bike yet?" Mike yelled.

"Can we ride it yet?" Max yelled.

"Hold on," Davey said. "Ben's still working on it. It's almost ready, but not yet."

"Why are the TV people back?" Max asked.

"Because Ben saw the monster again this morning," Davey answered.

Carrie stopped. "Maybe we should go tell Ben about the TV cameras," she said. "They might want to interview him."

"No!" Max and Mike both yelled at the same time.

"If he gets interviewed, he'll get famous,

and then he'll never put our bike back together again!" Mike explained. Max nodded.

"Don't worry," Nikki said. "Ben'll put your bike together." She stopped to think. "But maybe you're right. I think he probably does need all the time he can get to make sure it's ready for you."

Mike and Max nodded. They looked relieved.

"Where are you going?" Mike asked.

"We're going on a treasure hunt," Nikki said.

"Yeah?" Max said. "Can we come?"

"Sure."

"What's the treasure?" Mike asked.

"Bicycle parts," Carrie sniffed. "I'd prefer jewelry, myself."

"Bicycle parts are better than jewelry," Max sniffed, imitating Carrie. He nudged his brother.

The kids looked at the lake one last time. Then they decided who was going where to look for parts.

Nikki and Max and Mike were going to check out the vacant lot behind the grocery store. Davey agreed to look in the junkyard, and Carrie—who wasn't into dirt or garbage—volunteered to check out the bicycle shop.

"I bet once the guys in the repair shop know who I am—Carrie van de Hopper—" she said with one eyebrow raised, "they'll be so impressed, I'll get everything you guys need for free!"

"Sure . . ." Nikki said, half under her breath. "You're the princess of Appleby Corners. And you'll never let us forget it."

The group agreed to bring everything they found back to the park right away. If nobody found anything, they would meet at the park anyway at three o'clock.

As they left through the park's front gate, Nikki saw Wheels Gilligan rush by. He was carrying a strange black box that looked like an ugly radio.

Nikki wondered for a second what Wheels was up to now. But then she realized that she didn't have time to worry about Wheels Gilligan, or anything else for that matter. She was off on a treasure hunt!

CHAPTER
FOUR

Later that afternoon, Nikki, Mike, and Max almost ran back to Apple Park. Mike and Max were excited about the stuff they had found. They could hardly wait to see Ben.

But when they got to the gate, Nikki stopped them. She realized she had a big problem. Ben was fixing the twins' bike in the gazebo. But Mike and Max didn't know about the gazebo, or the Apple Park Gang. It was supposed to be a secret from everyone.

"I'll tell you what," she said. "Why don't you guys go down to the lake and watch for the monster? I'll take this stuff over to Ben's house."

"We want to watch Ben fix our bike," Mike said.

"That monster won't show up with so many people watching, anyway," Max said. "She's shy, remember? Let's just take this stuff to Ben's house."

What was Nikki going to do? She couldn't take the boys to the gazebo without letting out the secret. But now that she was baby-sitting them, Mike and Max spent so much time with her that she didn't have much choice.

Getting down on her knees, she looked first at one and then the other. "Can you boys keep a secret?" she said slowly.

Mike and Max looked very serious. "Yup."

"Well, Ben and Davey and Carrie and I all belong to a club called the Apple Park Gang."

Mike's and Max's eyes got round as saucers. "Wow!" Mike said.

"Can we join?" Max asked.

"Well," Nikki said slowly, "I don't know. I think you *might* be able to . . ."

"Neat!" Max cried.

". . . but not right away," Nikki finished. "First you have to keep this a secret until you're in second grade."

Both their faces fell.

"But that's next year!" Mike said.

"I know," Nikki said. "When you're in second grade, you'll be old enough. But you have to keep the gang a secret, and you have to keep our clubhouse a secret for a whole year. If you can do that . . . then next year you can be members!"

"Why do we have to keep it a secret?" Mike asked.

"Because," Nikki said, "what kind of a

club would it be if everybody knew all about it?"

The twins thought this over for a moment. Then they nodded. "Okay," Max said. "We'll keep the secret."

"But where's the clubhouse?" Mike asked. "We can't keep it a secret if we don't know where it is."

"I'll show you," Nikki said. "It's the old gazebo. That's where Ben is right now. He's fixing your bike in the clubhouse."

"Wow!" Max followed Nikki as if he were a puppy.

"This is sooo neat!" Mike lugged the bag of stuff they'd found in the vacant lot. "I can hardly wait to see the bike!"

But as they started toward the gazebo, Nikki noticed that Julia Forbes and her television crew had set up their camera and lights near the lake. They were interviewing the people who had gathered to look for the monster. It looked like everyone in Appleby Corners was there!

Nikki and the twins stopped to watch and listen, and they even got Julia Forbes to talk to them. But they did not like the interview one bit. They rushed to tell the gang what people were saying. When Nikki and the twins finally got to the gazebo, they found Davey and Carrie already there. Nikki was about to tell them what they'd discovered, but Carrie interrupted her.

"Hey!" Carrie pointed to the twins. "What are *they* doing here?"

"I told them about the club and the gazebo," Nikki said, frowning. Carrie's rudeness really made her mad. Carrie was the newest member of the gang, but sometimes she acted as if she had found the gazebo herself. "They can keep a secret, and besides, I think they should be members of the club when they get into second grade."

"No problem," Davey said. He patted Mike on the head. "They'd be good new members."

Mike and Max looked very happy.

Carrie sniffed as if she didn't care and turned to go inside the gazebo.

Nikki followed right behind her. "Ben!" she said as she stepped inside. "You wouldn't believe what people are saying out there!"

"Yeah!" said Mike and Max. They remembered what they'd heard in the park. "They're saying us kids made the whole thing up!"

Ben looked up from his work. "What do you mean?" he said.

Nikki sat down on the floor next to Ben. "We saw Julia Forbes out on the dock talking to Mr. P," she explained. "So we tried to get to her through the crowd."

"We shouted that we were the ones who saw the monster," Mike said.

"Right," Nikki said. "They all laughed at us, but they let us through anyway, and Julia

Forbes finally talked to us. The twins told her what they saw. We told her that Carrie had seen it too."

"And what did she say?" Davey asked.

"Well," Nikki went on, "Ms. Forbes listened to the story. Then she turned to the camera and said, 'It looks as if the only people who have actually seen Bessie the Lake Monster are all twelve years old and under. Maybe this monster only likes children, but we're all still wondering whether this monster exists at all.' "

"That's outrageous!" Carrie said. "You told her *I* saw it, and she didn't believe it? No van de Hopper has ever made anything up!"

Nikki thought about the trick Carrie had tried to play on the twins when she first pretended to see the lake monster. But Nikki didn't say anything. There was no point in getting into an argument with Carrie now.

"And Ms. Forbes wouldn't even listen to us after that," said Max. "We tried to tell her all about its long neck and humpy back, and she just patted me on the head!"

"And that's not all," said Nikki glumly. "After the TV crew left, I heard people saying that it was all a hoax so that your uncle could sell more hot dogs!"

Ben's face got red when he heard that. "That's a lie! My uncle would *never* do anything like that!"

"Everyone in this town is simply disgusting," Carrie said, sniffing. "They wouldn't even believe *me!* A *van de Hopper!*"

"Forget about that old monster. Look what we got!" Max dumped a pillowcase full of stuff on the ground.

"And I found two wheels," Davey said. "That junkyard is a gold mine!"

"Great," Ben said, looking at the wheels. "Just what I needed! But I still need a handle-bar stem, a head tube, a seat stay . . ."

"Look in our bag!" Mike said.

Ben opened the twins' bag. "Gee." He pulled out a long metal tube. "This is interesting. Plumbing pipes?"

"Will they fit?" Nikki asked. "Maybe we could just spray-paint them—no one would ever know."

Ben looked dubiously at the collection of old pipes. He turned them over and over in his hands. Letting out a big sigh, he started matching them up against the pile of bicycle parts on the floor.

"Well," Carrie said, looking down her nose at the plumbing parts. "I *personally* wouldn't ride any bike that was built out of old toilet pipes and orange juice cans, but at least I have something useful to add. I managed to get this!"

She reached into her purse, and held something out to Ben.

"*Brakes!*" he whooped. "Fantastic, Carrie! How'd you get them?"

"It just so happens that the owner of the bicycle shop owes my father a favor or something," Carrie said. "So he just gave these to me for free."

"Thanks a lot, Carrie." Ben gave her a big grin. "That was the one thing I was afraid of . . . no brakes. You're terrific!"

Carrie smiled back. "I know," she said with a superior smirk. But Nikki could tell that she really was relieved to have brought back something useful.

Nikki shook her head, wondering how someone could be so helpful and so nasty at the same time.

Ben fiddled with the new collection of parts while Mike and Max watched him, fascinated. He used one of the long pipes to connect the front wheel to the new back wheel.

"All I have to do is weld a few of these poles together," Ben said. "And then attach the brakes and the chain. Then you have . . . ta-dah! *Two bikes!*"

Mike and Max cheered, but Davey and Nikki looked a little puzzled.

Carrie stood with her hands on her hips. She didn't look at all convinced. "I'll believe it when I see it," she said.

"Maybe we should leave our club genius to work in peace," Davey said. "Let's head back out to the lake and watch for the monster."

"Good idea," Carrie said. "I'm bored. And there's no air in this silly box of a clubhouse."

Carrie went outside, followed by Nikki and Davey. Mike and Max stayed behind to watch Ben.

But as the three older kids walked toward the lake, they noticed some people giggling and pointing at them.

One man stopped them. "Are you the kids who thought up the monster hoax?" he said.

"It's no hoax," Davey said.

"Aw, come on," the man said. "It was a smart move, kids. How much did that hot dog man pay you to do that? And the kid with the T-shirts? Pretty good sales gimmick, huh?"

"It wasn't a sales gimmick!" Nikki said loudly. "It was real!"

"Sure. Whatever you say." The man laughed. "But you kids better get on home now. There's gonna be a thunderstorm tonight. That'll make it hard even for monsters to stay out!" He walked away.

"The nerve of that idiot!" Carrie said. "I saw that monster, and so did Mike and Max and Ben!"

"Yeah," Nikki said. "Four people seeing exactly the same thing. That does make it seem possible."

"Possible!" shrieked Carrie. "I'm not some kind of nut who goes around saying I've seen monsters in the lake! I saw it, and I know it's there!"

The three of them headed back to the gazebo. Suddenly, fresh air didn't seem so important anymore. They'd been accused of lying. And they didn't like it one bit.

Back inside, they were surprised to see Mike and Max and Ben staring miserably at the pile of bicycle pieces.

"What's wrong?" Davey asked.

"I told you so!" Max complained.

"You see! We were right!" Mike said. "It *is* impossible!"

"And now we don't have *any* bike!" said Max.

"All we have is a big pile of junk!"

Ben stuck his lower lip out thoughtfully. His eyes were all squinty.

"So I hit a little snag here," he said. "But I'm not going to be stopped by any small problems."

"Small problems!" Carrie said, her voice getting screechy. "That's not the only problem we have!"

"That's right," Davey said. "All the grown-ups think you guys made up the monster, and you didn't. You saw it, Carrie saw it. . . ."

"And we saw it too," Mike said. Max nodded.

"This is a serious problem," Nikki said thoughtfully.

"Well, there's one sure way to make them believe us," Davey said excitedly.

"What's that?" Nikki asked. She didn't like

the look in Davey's eyes. The rest of the gang was confused.

"Get proof!" Davey answered.

"That's right," Ben agreed, standing up.

"And how are we going to do that?" Carrie asked skeptically.

"We're going to camp out here all night and all day until we see that monster!" Davey said. "And we'll prove to everyone in Appleby Corners that the Apple Park Gang doesn't lie!"

CHAPTER
FIVE

"**H**ow can we do that?" Nikki asked. "We'll get tired."

"We'll need permission," Mike said.

"We'll get bugs crawling all over us!" Carrie said.

"And besides, there's supposed to be a storm tonight," said Nikki.

"Who cares about a little storm?" Ben said. "I know I saw that monster, and I don't like people accusing my uncle Frank of lying just to sell hot dogs!"

"You're right!" Carrie said. "I'll get my camera. It has a flash. We'll take a picture of Bessie. *Then* let them say the monster's not there!"

"How're we gonna stay awake?" Mike asked doubtfully.

"We'll take turns," Davey replied. "One will watch while the others sleep. Just like in the army!"

"We'll bring sleeping bags," Ben said. "Do all of you have sleeping bags?"

"Of course," Carrie sniffed. "I have an alpine, pure down sleeping bag. It's the best, you know. It's good for down to seventy degrees below zero."

"I don't think it's going to get colder than sixty degrees above zero tonight," Nikki said. Carrie could really be a pain sometimes.

"Then it's settled," Davey said. "All we have to do is get our sleeping bags . . ."

"And snacks," Carrie said.

"And permission," Ben said.

"What about our bikes?" Mike and Max howled.

"Don't worry," Ben said. "I think I can make it work. I'll fix them up as soon as we get back!"

The kids quickly made their way out of the park. They all went to their separate houses to get permission and useful things for the long night ahead.

But no more than five minutes went by before the phones in each house started ringing. Mike and Max called Nikki to say they weren't allowed to go at all. They were too young. Then Ben called Davey to tell him that Ben's father didn't care what people were saying, Ben couldn't stay in the park all night alone. Carrie's, Nikki's, and Davey's parents all said the same thing.

"Now what do we do?" Nikki asked Davey over the telephone.

The two of them decided not to give up. And after twelve more phone calls, the older kids' parents finally decided it was all right for them to camp out in the park if they had a chaperon.

Ben's father called Mr. P at his little gatekeeper's house at the edge of the park. Mr. P agreed to keep an eye on the kids.

But Mike and Max's parents wouldn't budge. "They still say we're too young," Max whimpered to Davey over the phone. "We have to wait until second grade. Why does everything have to wait till second grade, anyway?"

"Don't worry, Max," Davey said. "We'll give you a full report on what happens. And I'll make sure Ben takes care of your bike, okay?"

Meanwhile, the van de Hoppers said they would give the kids a picnic dinner. Nikki told Carrie she would help carry the food. Finally the Apple Park Gang was ready to get the *real* goods on Bessie the Lake Monster, and defend their good name!

When Nikki showed up at Carrie's house, she was amazed all over again. She'd been in Carrie's house before, but she was always surprised at how much the van de Hopper house looked like a mansion! In the kitchen the cook was packing a picnic hamper big enough to feed an army—not just four kids.

"Do you want to see my room?" Carrie asked.

"Sure," Nikki said. If Carrie's room was any-

thing like the rest of her house, it was going to be pretty incredible.

Carrie's room *was* incredible. There was a juke box in it, and a collection of stuffed animals that were practically life-size. Nikki remembered seeing ones like them at the giant toy store in New York City. Her parents had taken her there when she was little.

But Nikki was especially impressed by Carrie's computer. It was the latest computer with all the best programs! There was one that wrote music and another that did animation. It was fabulous.

"I didn't know you could use a computer!" Nikki said excitedly, walking over to look at it.

"I can't. I don't even know how to turn it on," said Carrie. "No one around here knows how to teach me."

"I can teach you," Nikki said. "It's just like my mom and dad's, but they don't have all those great programs. They cost too much."

"Would you really?" Carrie asked. "That would be great, Nikki."

"No problem," Nikki said. "We could figure out how to use all these programs together! I've always wanted to try these."

"It's neat that you know about computers." Carrie frowned, almost shyly. "Sometimes I wish I knew more practical stuff. Like how to fix bikes, or win bicycle races like Davey."

Nikki smiled. She had never seen Carrie

admit to wanting to be like anyone else before. She liked her better when she acted this way.

"It's easy to learn how to run a computer," she said. "And once you get started, there are all kinds of games and stuff you can do with it. Who knows," she added uncertainly when Carrie smiled gratefully at her. "We might even get to be friends."

Carrie grinned ruefully. "Well, yeah, I guess so," she said. "I never had a *real* friend . . . not like a best friend the way all the other girls have. I guess I'm not the easiest person to get along with."

"Oh, you're not so bad," Nikki couldn't help teasing. "Even if you *are* a van de Hopper!"

She laughed when Carrie threw a pillow at her. "Anyway, I'll tell you a secret," she said. "I never had a best friend, either." She smiled at Carrie's surprised look. "So let's shake on it. Computer pals forever! We'll start working on it tomorrow."

The two girls shook hands, and Nikki almost felt good about Carrie. Maybe Carrie acted so superior all the time because she didn't feel as useful as the others in the gang. Maybe they *could* be friends. She'd have to wait and see.

"Hey, let's get out of here." Carrie checked her gold wristwatch. "We've got a monster to spy on!"

CHAPTER SIX

The first half hour the kids spent on the lookout was fun. But after they'd eaten the fried chicken, the potato salad, the bean salad, the apple pie, and the cheese puffs (there were about five thousand cheese puffs left over from a cocktail party at the van de Hoppers'), there wasn't too much to do. Except listen to the wind howl, of course . . . and it was really howling.

"Who's going to go out and watch the lake first?" Ben asked.

"Not me," Carrie said. "Maybe I should collect all this stuff and put it away. Otherwise bugs will come and crawl all over us in the middle of the night."

"Are you sure you kids want to do this?" Mr. P grumbled sleepily. "It sounds like it's getting pretty wild out there."

He was right. The wind was whistling through the trees, making an eerie sound that gave Nikki the creeps.

"Well, since there's no big stampede of volunteers," Ben said, "I guess I'll go first."

Ben picked up Carrie's camera. "I'll be back in two hours," he said.

Ben wasn't gone for more than ten minutes when the rest of them heard a suspicious plopping noise on the roof of the clubhouse.

"Rain!" Carrie said softly.

Within seconds the rain started coming down in torrents. Ben burst through the door, shaking water off himself and onto everyone else.

"You can't see anything out there," he announced. "It feels like a big bucket of water just got poured down on Apple Park. I couldn't take a picture in this rain even if I *could* see the lake!"

"Well, we'll wait awhile," Davey said calmly. "It's bound to stop soon."

But the rain went on and on . . . and on. The sound of it drumming on the wooden platform over their heads lulled the kids to sleep. One by one, their eyes closed. Soon, not one person in the clubhouse was awake.

They didn't sleep for very long. Suddenly there was an explosion of noise, and all four kids shot out of their sleeping bags and huddled in the middle of the room.

"What was that?" Carrie screeched.

There was a long, low rumble followed by another huge clap of booming noise.

"Boy, that's what I call thunder," said Ben.

"Boy!" Davey looked at Mr. P, who hadn't moved a muscle or stopped snoring. "That's what I call sleeping!"

Then there was another, different sort of crash—right next to the gazebo!

"*That* wasn't thunder." Nikki's voice trembled.

"It sounded like a tree branch falling," Davey said. "It must have hit the roof of the gazebo."

"I don't like this," Carrie said.

"Me neither," Nikki said. "But there isn't much we can do about it. We'll just have to wait it out."

It was impossible to go to sleep with the storm raging outside. The kids sat up and listened to the thunder and the sound of Mr. P snoring.

Finally, out of sheer boredom, Ben asked Davey to aim the flashlight at his bicycle work area for him.

"I might as well do something useful," Ben said. He started fitting the bike parts together.

For some strange reason, this time the parts fit together as smooth as butter. It took a bit of help from each member of the Apple Park Gang, but in an hour Ben had transformed the tandem bike for two into two separate bikes for one!

"Wait till the twins see this. You're a genius, Ben," Davey said.

"Well, I wouldn't say he's a genius," Carrie said, looking at the bike. "But that *is* pretty good!"

"So maybe he's not a genius," Nikki said. "Maybe he's only brilliant! But that's good enough for me!"

Now that they'd worked on the twins' bike, there wasn't anything for them to do but listen to the rain. Though the thunder had finally stopped, they could still hear the wind gusting just as hard. Rain drummed steadily on the clubhouse roof.

"So much for catching the lake monster." Ben yawned as he snuggled down into his sleeping bag. "I'll get a little sleep, and then when the rain stops, I'll go back out . . . it can't go on much longer."

"Maybe we should keep watch again tomorrow night," Nikki said, her eyes closing despite themselves.

"No," Ben said. "It's got to stop soon."

But it didn't. Soon they were all asleep again, and it was quiet in the gazebo—except, of course, for an occasional snort from the sleeping Mr. P.

As the first shafts of light came filtering through the cracks between the boards of the gazebo, Nikki woke up. She opened the back door and saw that the sun was just rising. A strange, pearly glow was on the lake. It was still very cloudy, but the gray clouds had a pink cast to them.

"Hey, guys!" she said, shaking Ben's shoulder. "It's morning!"

"Oh, no." Ben rubbed his eyes. "We slept all night long! What time is it?"

"My watch says five-thirty," Davey said.

"Ugh." Carrie yawned. "I've never been up at five-thirty in the morning in my entire life! I feel awful!"

"Is it still raining out there?" Ben sat up in his sleeping bag.

"No," Nikki said. "But it's pretty windy."

Carrie buried her face in her sleeping bag. Mr. P continued to doze noisily.

"Let's have a look." Nikki stepped outside. Her jacket almost blew off as a gust of wind caught her by surprise. Wow! It really *is* windy out here! she thought.

She started to walk down toward the lake. Then she stopped suddenly. She turned and sprinted silently back to the gazebo.

"Shhhhhhh!" she hissed as she joined the others. "I just saw Wheels Gilligan down by the lake!"

"What's *he* doing down there?" Carrie whispered.

"I don't know," Nikki said. "But let's sneak down and find out!"

Walking as quickly and as quietly as they could, Nikki, Ben, Davey, and Carrie made their way down to a clump of bushes near where Wheels Gilligan stood at the end of the dock. They watched, open-mouthed, as he reached into a little bag and pulled out a small black box. He pulled up an antenna that was on the top of the contraption.

"It's a remote control box!" Davey whispered.

Wheels twiddled a few dials on the remote. Suddenly, to the kids' astonishment, Bessie the Lake Monster surfaced on the lake. She moved majestically along as Wheels used the hand controls on the remote.

"It *is* a phony!" Carrie whispered, her voice sharp with indignation.

"Shhhhh!" Ben said.

"We should have known all along," Nikki muttered. "I mean, how did he get all those souvenirs and T-shirts printed up in such a hurry?"

"That's right!" Davey said. "I'll bet he's been planning this for weeks!"

"And to think everybody blamed us!" Nikki snapped. "And Uncle Frank too."

"We ought to go right down there and punch that rat-faced bully in the nose," Carrie said. "After all, not only is *my* honor at stake as a van de Hopper, but the honor of this gang is at stake too!"

Carrie started to march out from behind the shrubbery when Davey clapped his hand on her shoulder and pulled her back down.

"Not now!" he whispered. "Let's see if we can get hold of his equipment. That's the only way we can prove it was a hoax."

". . . and prove that Wheels Gilligan was

the one who pulled it off too," Nikki said softly. "After all, everyone thinks it's a hoax already. All we want to prove is that we didn't do it!"

Davey nodded. "Let's just sit tight until we can figure out a way to nail him."

The kids watched from behind the bush as Wheels twiddled the dials and sent "Bessie" all over the lake. The more they watched, the madder they got.

"We should get Wheels *and* that inflated monster thing too. The more proof we have, the better off we'll be," Nikki said.

"Did you see him put it in the water?" Davey asked Nikki.

"Nope," she replied. "All I saw was when he opened up the bag and took out the remote."

"Maybe he keeps the thing hidden somewhere for the night," Ben said. "If we watch long enough, we'll see exactly where he sends it."

"Well, I certainly hope he stops practicing soon," Carrie said. "I'm starving."

"Me too," Ben said. "Carrie, why don't you go get us some cheese puffs? There must be about four thousand left."

"Good thinking," Davey said. "And hurry back."

Carrie wasn't used to the idea of being ordered around, and glared at the two boys. But when they turned back to watch Wheels with his fake monster, she gave up, shrugged, and started off.

Because Carrie didn't want Wheels to see her, she backed out of the bushes and then scrambled off crablike toward the gazebo. She looked like a soldier running low across an open field. Nikki, Ben, and Davey watched Carrie's weird movements. It was all they could do to keep from laughing.

"I can't believe she's actually going to get the cheese puffs," Davey said.

"Me neither," Ben said. "Maybe she feels sick."

"I think she's trying to be useful," Nikki said.

"What makes you say that?" Davey asked.

"She told me that it bothers her not to have anything useful to do in the gang," Nikki explained.

"Really?" Ben said.

Nikki explained about the conversation she'd had with Carrie. "Maybe she'll get tired of being nice," she said. "But at least for now she's trying to help out."

"Good," Davey said. "Especially since I'm starving!"

They turned their attention back to the lake. Wheels was acting very peculiar all of a sudden. Before, Bessie had been gliding around the lake, diving and surfacing. But now she had gone down for a dive and hadn't come up. And Wheels was shaking his remote control box and cursing. He shook it a few more times, and then threw it down on the dock.

"Oh, no," Davey said. "It looks like his remote is broken, or he's lost Bessie."

"If Wheels loses her, we'll never be able to prove anything!" Nikki said.

"Now what's he doing?" Carrie had reappeared with a huge plastic bag full of cheese puffs. "How come Wheels looks so mad?"

"He's lost Bessie," Davey explained. "He can't make the remote control work on her."

"Now it looks like he's going to take one of the boats out," Ben said.

Wheels stomped back to the boat house, and lowered himself down into one of the boats. He yanked at the ropes and then finally released one of the boats from its mooring at the dock. Grabbing the oars stowed on the bottom, Wheels began rowing furiously out into the middle of the lake.

The gusty wind was making pretty big waves out on the lake. The little boat smacked up and down with each wave. Sometimes the prow lifted so high out of the water that the oars didn't even touch. Wheels was having a hard time controlling the little boat, but he kept rowing as hard as he could.

When he was thirty feet out onto the lake, the wind picked up even more. A few big round drops of water started to rain down on the kids.

"I hope he finds that dumb monster soon," Carrie muttered nervously. "My hair gets the frizzies whenever I'm out in the rain for more than thirty seconds."

"Forget about the frizzies," Ben said irritably. "This is an undercover operation!"

"It's only an undercover operation if he can find Bessie," Carrie pointed out. "If he can't, then I guess we're all sunk."

As soon as Carrie said the word "sunk," a terrible thing happened.

Wheels was standing crouched at the back of the boat when, suddenly, the prow of the little rowboat lifted high in the air. With a horrible lurch the boat flipped over onto its side.

As the gang watched, Wheels stumbled and flapped his arms wildly. Then he fell smack into the lake.

CHAPTER
SEVEN

"**H**e'll drown!" Nikki shouted.

"We've got to save him!" Ben yelled.

"Get another rowboat," Davey cried. "Come on!"

"Are you kidding?" Carrie said. "We'll drown ourselves out there in this weather. I say we call the police instead!"

Ben didn't take the time to argue. "All right, you stay here," he said, already running for the boat house. "Keep an eye on us!"

"If Wheels owes us his life," Nikki agreed, scanning the lake for him, "maybe he'll confess on TV and save us the trouble of trying to find Bessie."

"Don't bet on it with Wheels," Davey said. "He's not known for doing anything nice for *anyone* . . . no matter *what* they've done for him." He took off after Ben. Nikki followed.

"I say we should just let him drown," Carrie called after them. "He's too mean to save!"

But they weren't listening. Instead, they were already climbing into a rowboat. Carrie grumbled to herself and started toward the dock to keep watch.

Davey and Ben sat next to each other on the boat's middle seat. They both pulled hard on the oars. Nikki sat in the back, holding on to both sides of the boat. They made their way slowly across the lake to the spot where Wheels' boat had capsized.

The choppy water hit the prow, splashing everyone. But it didn't matter. The rain was coming down hard again, anyway.

"Hang on, Wheels!" Davey called over his shoulder, rowing with all his might. "We're coming!"

Nikki searched the lake for any sign of Wheels near his overturned boat. It was hard to see through the rain. She thought she saw an arm clinging to the prow, but she couldn't be sure.

"Will you look at the size of these waves?" Davey shouted to Ben. "It feels like every time we go forward two feet, the waves push us back three feet."

"I know," said Ben, rowing hard. "We'd be better off with surfboards!"

By the time they reached Wheels's rowboat their clothes were stuck to their skin, and their hair was plastered down on their heads. Nikki scanned the other boat's wet surface.

Wheels wasn't there. They didn't see him anywhere.

"Wheels!" Ben shouted into the rain. He peered out across the choppy gray water. "Where are you?"

Suddenly, a pair of hands grabbed the side of their boat. A wet face peeked over the top. It looked as pale and as slick as a hard-boiled egg.

"Save me!" Wheels screamed. "There's a monster down here!"

"Sure," Davey said. "Bessie the Lake Monster!"

"It's trying to eat me!" Wheels shrieked. He tried to pull himself into their rowboat, but his feet kept slipping on its slippery side. "It's bumping my legs!"

"Come off it, Wheels," Nikki said. "Quit trying to fool everyone."

"Stop screaming and flapping around so much," Davey said. "We'll help you in."

Davey steadied the boat with his oars. Ben and Nikki pulled Wheels up by his hands. Wheels jumped in so fast he almost overturned the boat.

"Slow down!" Ben yelled. "You'll have us all in the lake if you don't watch it."

Wheels lay on the bottom of the boat for a minute, his sides heaving. Then he slowly looked up at them.

"Listen, I swear," he said, "there's a monster out there. That's how come my boat overturned."

"You stood up in your boat," Nikki said. "That's why it overturned. Anyone with half a brain knows not to stand up in a rowboat."

"Especially when it's choppy," Ben said. "And you can stop with the monster stuff too. We know the truth, Wheels. We saw you with that fancy remote control unit."

For a moment it looked like Wheels turned even paler. Then he frowned and sat up. "Okay," he said. "I admit it. I did use an inflatable monster with a remote."

Nikki, Ben, and Davey exchanged triumphant looks. Grinning, Davey took up his oars and began rowing back toward the shore.

"But wait!" Wheels screeched. "I swear there's something *real* out there! It hit my boat just as I was reaching over to grab Bessie. Really! And then when I was in the water, it kept bumping me. It came back again and again. . . ."

Wheels started shaking. Nikki noticed that he was crying too.

"You're just cold," Ben said grimly, starting to row. "You'll be okay when we get you to shore."

"Hurry," Wheels sniveled. "Before the monster overturns this boat too!"

Nikki laughed and shook her head. She looked at Davey, and he grinned back. His look said, *He's gone totally nuts.*

"Should we try to tow in the other boat?" Nikki asked as they passed it in the water.

"No, please!" Wheels cried. "Puhlleeze, let's get out of here!"

Ben grinned. He enjoyed seeing a bully like Wheels act a little less tough for a change. "We can always come back for it later," he said to the other two. They kept the boat aimed toward the shore.

This time the waves were working with them rather than against them, and they made it back quickly.

As they pulled up to the dock, Nikki looked around for Carrie. She wasn't there.

"So much for letting Carrie watch out for us," Nikki said. "She's gone."

"She probably went inside to keep her hair from getting wet," Davey grumbled. "It doesn't matter. Let's get onshore."

Soaking wet from the rain and the waves, the three of them helped Wheels out of the boat, then ran for cover under the boat house. They certainly couldn't take Wheels to the gazebo. He was the last person on earth they wanted to have find out about their clubhouse.

In the boat house Ben found an old tarp. He draped it over them as protection against the rain dripping solidly off the eaves of the shack. It didn't work very well, though. The wind kept flipping up the corners.

"Let's sit here and wait it out," Ben said. "It looks like the sky is starting to clear, so it shouldn't be too long now."

"You've been saying that all night," Davey said with a smile. Then he turned to Wheels. "Now tell us the truth about the monster."

"I *am* telling you the truth," Wheels said through chattering teeth. "I *did* use my remote control unit to make a rubber sea monster swim all over the place. But that was yesterday and the day before." He wiped the tears from his face.

"Today, when I went out there with my remote," he went on, "it stopped working. I couldn't get Bessie out of a dive. I went out in the rowboat to get the blowup monster and bring it back to shore because I figured the attachment that picked up the radio waves was loose or something."

"Why did you do it in the first place?" Nikki interrupted angrily. "What was the point of getting all those people so excited?"

"I didn't mean to, at first." Wheels hesitated for a second. "But then I saw the way those twins you baby-sit and that rich girl, Carrie, screamed when they saw it. And I figured it would be fun to see how much I could scare other people." He grinned. "And then I figured out a way to make money off it too," he bragged.

"The T-shirts," Nikki muttered. She had known all along there was something suspicious about them.

"So what makes you think there was something real out there now?" Ben asked.

"When I went out there in the boat, I thought I saw Bessie. I stood up so I could grab hold of her and pull her into the boat. That's when I felt something knock hard against the bottom of the boat. It lifted the front end up in the air. I fell over, and the boat went over with me. . . ."

"It could have been the wind," Nikki said.

"No," Wheels said, shaking his head so hard his wet hair stood out in spikes. "I've been out in boats on that lake my whole life, and it wasn't the wind."

Wheels's eyes were wide as he remembered what had happened. He looked as if he were about to cry again. Nikki watched him, fascinated. Wheels was one of the toughest kids in town. He usually scared *other* people. Even dogs were scared of Wheels. If something had scared *him* then it must be pretty scary.

"How do you know it wasn't something else?" Nikki asked. She wasn't the type of person who would easily believe in things like monsters. "After all, it could have been just a big fish."

"It wasn't, I tell you!" Wheels screamed at her. "There's something out there! I'm never going out on that lake again!"

Davey stood up, but he was a little worried about Wheels's story. He wasn't the kind to break down and cry at the drop of a hat. Maybe there actually *was* a monster in Apple Park Lake. . . .

Just then Mr. P came around the front of the boat house. "Well," he said with a strange smile on his face. "What're you kids doing up in the park so early?"

Davey, Ben, and Nikki smiled back, relieved that he didn't let on to Wheels where they'd all spent the night.

"We were looking for a monster," Davey said. "And Wheels found one!"

"Oh, really?" Mr. P's bushy eyebrows shot up on his forehead.

Wheels was still shaking. "It's out there, Mr. P—honest!" he said. "It tried to eat me!"

"Did it really, now?" Mr. P looked Wheels up and down with an amused expression on his face.

"Maybe we should tell you the whole story first," Nikki said. She told him about seeing Wheels guiding Bessie around the lake with the remote control.

"But that's not the monster I'm talking about," Wheels blubbered. "There's a real one out there, too, besides the one I put out there."

When Wheels told Mr. P what had happened, the park keeper looked out onto the lake. He saw one of his rowboats out there upside down. He frowned.

"So you kids took my boats out there without my permission?" he asked sternly.

The three members of the Apple Park Gang looked sheepish.

"But Mr. P," Nikki said. "We had to save Wheels!"

"Yes, of course. You did the right thing," Mr. P said. "But I never want to hear of anyone taking one of my boats like that again. It's much too dangerous."

He turned back to Wheels. "As far as this monster goes, I think your imagination just got all worked up because of your own trickery. Probably what bumped against your legs was a tree limb and nothing more."

"It was slimy and soft!" Wheels said in a high-pitched whine. "Tree limbs don't feel like that!"

"It could have been soft from having been in the water for a long time," said Mr. P firmly. "Now, I think that's enough. I want you all to go home and get into dry clothes. We'll tell everyone in Apple Park what happened—and who started it—later today."

Mr. P took off his cap and shook it. Some raindrops and a few leaves fell out.

"I'm ready for a good breakfast," he said with a weary smile. Then he turned and marched into the boat house, closing the door behind him.

"Me too," Ben said. "Let's head on home."

They hadn't gone two feet when they saw Mike come barreling into the park. He was out of breath and seemed very upset.

"Ben!" he yelled when he got up to them

even though his mouth was about six inches from Ben's ear. "Something terrible's happened!"

"What's wrong?" Ben held on to Mike's shoulders. "Where's Max?"

But Mike wasn't looking at him anymore. He was staring straight ahead out onto the lake.

"Hey!" Mike said with a big smile. "There's Bessie!"

The four older kids spun around. Sure enough, out on the lake was a big, glistening hump, gliding smoothly through the water.

"That can't be Bessie," Nikki cried. "Bessie's broken, at the bottom of the lake."

"There really *is* something out there!" Ben shouted.

That was all Wheels had to hear. He screamed and raced out of the park as if the monster itself were right behind him.

CHAPTER
EIGHT

Neato!" Mike said as the hump moved closer to their side of the lake. They could see the tiny head and long, slender neck. "Too bad Max missed seeing Bessie again. He'll be really mad when I tell him."

"I can't believe it," Ben said. "Wheels was right!"

"That's not Bessie," Davey said. "So it has to be . . . it has to be *real*!"

"I don't believe I'm seeing this," Nikki said.

But there it was, as plain as day. A real live lake monster was slowly circling Apple Park Lake.

Nikki felt shivers go up and down her spine. She blinked, trying to believe what she was seeing. What was a prehistoric monster doing in their lake?

"Hey, Ben!" Mike said, suddenly remembering something. He yanked hard on Ben's sleeve to get his attention. "Forget about the monster for a minute! Something terrible's happened!"

Ben, never taking his eyes off the lake, croaked, "What's up? What happened that was so terrible?"

"Great-Aunt Amelia's here on a visit!"

"*What!*" they all cried together. "You mean here in Apple Park?"

"No, not in the park, silly," Mike said. "At our house. She wants to see us riding the new bike!"

"Uh-oh," Ben said. "Well—I have good news and bad news."

Mike's face fell. "I don't like bad news. Tell me the good news," he said in a tiny voice.

"It's the same as the bad news, Mike," Nikki said. "Last night Ben turned the tandem into two bikes for you guys."

There was dead silence on the edge of the lake as the four of them stared at Mike. His face started to collapse, and his bottom lip stuck out.

"Oh, brother," he said sadly. "Now we're *really* in a big mess."

He slowly picked up his foot and kicked as hard as he could at a little rock that lay nearby.

The rock flew into a clump of bushes by the boat house.

The bush started to shake, and they all heard a loud "Ouch!"

Four heads snapped around to look in the direction of the "ouch."

The bushes shook even harder, and suddenly Carrie stepped out. She was holding her ankle with one hand, and a big black box in the other.

"Who's the dirty little rat who threw that rock at me?" she snapped, glaring at Mike.

"Oh, boy, I'm sorry," Mike said, backing away. "I didn't even know you were—"

"Yeah!" Ben said. "Nobody knew you were in that bush, Ms. van de Hopper."

"And just what, exactly, were you doing in that bush?" Davey pointed to the black box Carrie held in her hand.

Carrie grinned mischievously.

"That looks suspiciously like a remote control unit," said Nikki. She stepped closer to Carrie so she could get a good look at the black box.

"It just so happens you're right," Carrie said triumphantly. "I thought it might be fun to give Wheels a little scare."

"And maybe a few other people too?" Ben asked.

Carrie's smile started to falter.

"Where'd you get that?" Mike pulled the contraption out of Carrie's hand. "Wow! This is a big one!"

"Yeah, Carrie," Davey said. "Where'd *you* get a remote control unit like that?"

Nikki, Ben, and Davey all stood with their arms folded across their chests, waiting for Carrie to explain.

Carrie looked at their serious faces. She giggled. "Well, there I was sitting on the dock watching you guys trying to row back to shore with Wheels, and I had an idea! I thought if I ran home as quick as I could, I might be able to get this unit and give old Wheels the scare of his life before he left the park!"

"I didn't know you liked radio control stuff!" Ben said.

"Are you kidding?" Carrie said. "I hate it. But I have this crazy uncle who always brings me big expensive toys from his trips. He can't remember whether I'm a boy or a girl, or how old I am, either. Once he brought me a four-foot African mask and a Bombay taxi horn—is that stupid, or what? And once he even brought me a stuffed monkey. Yecch!"

The other kids stared at Carrie.

"Anyway," she went on, "he brought me this remote control boat from Japan. He said it would go fifty miles an hour on open water. We tried it in the pool. It went fifty miles an hour all right . . . right into the edge! The remote control unit is still okay, but the boat is sort of a mess!"

"So you figured it just might work on Wheels's monster," Davey said, starting to grin.

"Right!" Carrie said, smiling. "And it did, didn't it?"

"It sure did," Nikki said, starting to laugh. "I bet he won't be much of a problem for a while!"

"What about the bike?" Mike said, yanking hard on Ben's sleeve. "What am I supposed to do?"

"Well, er . . . why don't you just tell Great-Aunt Amelia you have a little surprise for her?" Ben looked a little uncomfortable.

"I can't!" Mike wailed. His face started to crumple up again.

"Hey! Don't cry," Ben said quickly. "I'll go put it all back together right now. Okay?"

Mike's face uncrumpled, and a smile appeared. "Can you really?"

"Sure he can," Nikki added. "But he'll need a little time."

"How long?" Mike asked. "She said she was going to come down to the park so me and Max could show her how well we can ride. She said she was coming now!"

"Now?" Davey said.

"Now!" Mike said. "Well, not *right* now. Max is showing her our ant farm first."

"How long can you look at an ant farm?" Nikki asked.

"Not that long," Ben said, frowning. "I'm not sure I can—"

"Hey, guys," Carrie said, tapping Ben on the shoulder. "I have a plan."

"You do?" Nikki looked at Carrie.

"Let's have Mike wait for his great-aunt Amelia and Max at the park gate," Carrie said. "He can bring them down here to the lake, and I'll make Bessie do tricks for them. That'll keep Great-Aunt Amelia busy for a while, and it'll give Ben a chance to put the bike back together again."

Nikki smiled. "It just might work!"

"Sure it will!" Ben whooped. "I'm starting now. I'll whistle when it's ready!"

Ben sprinted off around the park. He disappeared into the bushes behind the gazebo.

"Now you go meet Great-Aunt Amelia and Max," Nikki said. "And remember . . . make sure they walk slow!"

Mike ran out of the park as fast as his legs could carry him.

Carrie and Nikki sat down by the edge of the lake to wait for Great-Aunt Amelia and the boys. Unfortunately for Ben, they didn't have to wait very long. In fact, Nikki could hardly believe her eyes when Great-Aunt Amelia came swinging along into the park. Mike and Max looked like they were having a hard time keeping up with her.

She was a tiny woman with a smooth pink face and sparkly blue eyes. Her hair was pulled back into a long white braid.

"Wait up!" Mike called to Great-Aunt Amelia.

"Here's our friends Nikki and Carrie," Max said in between huffs and puffs.

"Hello, Nikki and Carrie," Great-Aunt Amelia said.

"Hello," Nikki said. She hoped Ben was hurrying. "Um, we've got something great to show you."

"It's the biggest thing that's happened in this town in fifty years," Carrie said.

She held out the little black box, twiddled the dials, and suddenly Bessie the Lake Monster surfaced and started swimming around the lake.

"Ah-ha!" said Great-Aunt Amelia, raising her eyebrows. "So you're the people who had everyone in town thinking there was a prehistoric monster in here, eh?"

"Not exactly," Nikki said.

They told Great-Aunt Amelia, Mike, and Max the whole story of Wheels, and how they caught him in the act, and how Carrie scared the living daylights out of the toughest kid in town.

Max and Mike were amazed to hear the whole story. Great-Aunt Amelia was thrilled. She wanted to try out Bessie for herself. Carrie handed over the remote control.

As soon as Great-Aunt Amelia got the hang of the box, Nikki bent down to Max. "Quick!" she whispered. "Go find out if Ben's ready yet!"

Max was back in two minutes looking miserable and shaking his head.

"Let me show you how to make Bessie dive," Carrie said helpfully.

That really got Great-Aunt Amelia's attention. She had Bessie gliding and diving all around the lake for another half hour.

"Go check again," Nikki hissed.

Max was back two minutes later. He shook his head again. "Five more minutes," he whispered.

"Here! Let me show you how to make Bessie do flips," Carrie said, snatching the remote control box. Great-Aunt Amelia had a great time making the sea monster alternate between flips and dives. In no time at all, they heard Ben's long, low whistle from the gazebo.

Mike and Max dodged into the bushes, and came out riding the bicycle built for two. Great-Aunt Amelia watched as the two of them made their unsteady, wobbling way around the park for her.

"It's perfect for them, isn't it?" she said to Nikki.

"Yes, it certainly is," Nikki answered.

"I have always known exactly the right present to give little boys," Great-Aunt Amelia said with a self-satisfied grin. "That's probably because I always wished I were a boy myself."

Carrie and Nikki exchanged a grin as Great-Aunt Amelia went back to playing with the remote.

*   *   *

Later that afternoon, the gang met at Carrie's house for snacks.

"Thank goodness there aren't any more cheese puffs," said Davey, diving into his third slice of pizza.

"I can't believe I got that bike apart and back together again," Ben said, shaking his head.

"And just right too," Nikki said.

"And just in time," Carrie added. "I couldn't have kept Great-Aunt Amelia busy too much longer. Even a lake monster begins to get boring after a while."

"What was it she said when she saw Bessie?" Nikki asked, giggling.

"She said Bessie reminded her of her sister. A long, pretty neck but not much of a brain." Carrie laughed.

"What a thing to say about your own sister," Nikki giggled.

"Great-Aunt Amelia has a bit of a mean streak, I guess," Ben said. "But I kind of liked her."

"I did too," Nikki said. "It's true that she's . . ."

"Eccentric," Carrie said.

"Right," Nikki went on. "Eccentric . . . or weird, like Mike and Max said. But nice. Eccentric and nice . . . and funny too!"

Then Ben raised his can of soda. "Speaking of eccentric, I say we make a toast to Carrie! Our newest member!"

The other kids cheered and raised their sodas.

"To Carrie!" they all said in unison. "Our newest member ... and the only person in Appleby Corners who can scare the pants off Wheels Gilligan!"

"Hurray!!"

Carrie's face glowed with happiness as she raised her own can of soda. "To the Apple Park Gang," she answered. "The best club in the whole wide world!"